Walt Disney's Cinderella

Illustrated by the Disney Storybook Artists
Story adapted by Amy Adair

© Disney Enterprises, Inc.

Published by
Louis Weber, C.E.O.
Publications International, Ltd.
7373 North Cicero Avenue
Lincolnwood, Illinois 60712

www.pilbooks.com

Manufactured in China.

8 7 6 5 4 3 2 1

ISBN: 0-7853-9776-0

Once upon a time there lived a very sweet girl named Cinderella. She was so beautiful that her stepmother and two stepsisters, Anastasia and Drizella, were filled with jealousy. They were extremely cruel to Cinderella and treated the poor girl like a servant.

Chirp, chirp, chirp! Early every morning bluebirds woke Cinderella from her slumber. Cinderella was always happy in the morning because she would spend the entire night dreaming about finding true love. Cinderella always sang in the morning. The mice came out of their little houses behind the walls just to listen to her. Two mice named Jaq and Gus were especially fond of Cinderella. They never missed her morning song.

All of the other animals that lived on the cottage grounds also adored Cinderella. She was kind and sweet to them, too. They looked forward to seeing her every morning when she gave them breakfast.

Cinderella's rude stepsisters always interrupted her peaceful mornings.

"Hurry up!" one stepsister yelled.

"What's taking so long?" the other cried.

Cinderella did not want to upset her stepsisters. She raced around the kitchen. She served her stepmother and stepsisters breakfast in bed every morning. They got very angry if she ever was late. Cinderella balanced the trays and climbed the steps to the bedrooms.

"Good morning, Drizella," Cinderella said kindly. Drizella grabbed a tray. Then she ordered Cinderella to iron a basketful of clothes.

Next, Cinderella went into Anastasia's room. "It's about time," Anastasia complained. "Don't forget to do the mending today."

Finally, Cinderella went into her stepmother's room. "Clean the carpets, then wash all the windows and drapes," her stepmother ordered. "When you're done with that, tend to the garden and clean the chimney."

Every day was exactly the same for Cinderella. She cooked, cleaned, ironed, and sewed from dawn to dusk.

Meanwhile, the King worried that his son, the Prince, would never find a suitable wife. He ordered his Grand Duke to throw a ball and invite all the eligible maidens in the entire kingdom. That very day, the Grand Duke sent a messenger out to every single house in the kingdom.

Cinderella was mopping the floors when the messenger knocked on her door.

"This is an urgent message from the King," he said, handing Cinderella an envelope. Cinderella knew it was important, so she gave it to her stepmother right away.

"This is an invitation to a royal ball!" the Stepmother shouted with joy. "By royal command, every eligible maiden should attend."

"What shall I wear?" Drizella asked.

"I can't wait to meet the Prince!" said Anastasia.

Cinderella was so excited she thought her heart would burst. "That means I can go!" she exclaimed.

The Stepmother looked at Cinderella, then smiled. "I see no reason why you can't go," the Stepmother said slyly. "That is, if you get all your work done and you can find something suitable to wear."

Cinderella didn't have any fancy clothes. But she did
have an old pink dress. She knew she could fix it so it
would be fit to wear to the Prince's ball. Cinderella raced
to her room and pulled the dress out of her trunk. She got
out her needle and thread, but before she could finish one
stitch her stepsisters called to her.

"Do my mending!" one yelled.

"Where are my slippers?" the other asked.

Jaq and Gus knew that poor Cinderella would never be able to finish her dress in time for the ball, so they called the other mice and birds. They all wanted to help and set right to work, sewing delicate lace and beautiful bows onto the old dress.

Jaq and Gus wanted Cinderella to have the prettiest dress at the entire ball. So they snuck downstairs and found an old pink sash and some beads that the stepsisters had thrown away. They were the perfect finishing touches for Cinderella's dress.

Before
Cinderella
knew it, the
clock chimed eight
times. Her stepmother and
stepsisters had kept her busy all day. She never
had a minute to spare to work on her own dress.

"Aren't you coming to the ball?" the Stepmother asked
cruelly. Cinderella shook her head and hid her tears. Then
she ran back to her room. She sadly stared out the window
and wished with all her heart that she could go to the ball.

Tweet! Tweet! The birds sang excitedly. They proudly
showed Cinderella her dress.

She could hardly believe how beautiful it was.

Cinderella quickly got dressed. "Wait for me!" she yelled to her stepmother as she flew down the steps. "I'm ready! I can go!"

Cinderella was absolutely stunning. She looked just like a real princess. The stepsisters were instantly filled with jealousy. "Those are my beads!" Drizella exclaimed, yanking them off Cinderella.

"That's my sash!" Anastasia yelled, pulling it off the dress. The stepsisters ruined Cinderella's beautiful dress. She couldn't possibly go to the ball now.

The Stepmother smiled. "Goodnight," she said, closing the door.

Cinderella ran to the garden and sobbed.

Suddenly, Cinderella's Fairy Godmother appeared. "Dry your tears," she gently told Cinderella. "You can't go to the ball like that."

Cinderella looked at her with surprise. "How can I go to the ball?"

The Fairy Godmother smiled. Then she waved her wand. A pumpkin appeared, and it grew and grew and grew until it was a carriage.

Then the Fairy Godmother pointed her magic wand at four mice. *Poof!* They now were gallant white horses. Then she turned to Cinderella's old friends, the horse and the dog. She magically turned them into a coachman and a footman.

"What about my dress?" Cinderella asked shyly.

The Fairy Godmother smiled. With one wave of her wand she turned Cinderella's dress into a ball gown and her shoes into elegant glass slippers.

Cinderella twirled around. She had never seen anything so beautiful.

"This is just like a dream!" she exclaimed happily.

"Like all dreams, this one cannot last forever," the Fairy Godmother explained. "At the stroke of midnight, the spell will be broken, and everything will be as it was before."

Cinderella was very nervous when she arrived at the ball. But as soon as the Prince saw Cinderella, he fell in love with her. They danced every single dance together.

Everyone admired the beautiful young woman that had captured the Prince's heart.

"Who is she?" people asked.

"I've never seen her before," someone whispered.

Cinderella's stepmother was furious that the Prince had not danced with her two daughters. She stared at the mysterious beauty who floated across the dance floor with the Prince. Something seemed strangely familiar about her.

As soon as the clock struck midnight, Cinderella remembered the Fairy Godmother's warning. "I must go home," she said, running out of the ballroom.

The Prince chased her. "Wait! How will I find you?"

Cinderella dashed down the palace steps. She was in such a hurry that she didn't even notice she had left one of her glass slippers behind.

On the last stroke of midnight, Cinderella's carriage turned back into a pumpkin. The horses were mice once again, the footman was a dog again, and her coachman was her old friend, the horse. Cinderella's beautiful dress even turned back into rags. She looked down at her feet. She was delighted to see that she still had one glass slipper.

"I'm sorry," she told her animal friends. "I must have forgotten all about the time." Cinderella couldn't help but think about the handsome man she had danced with all night long. It was the most wonderful night of her entire life. She stared at the glass slipper. It would always be a reminder of the one night that she felt like a true princess.

"Thank you, Fairy Godmother," she whispered.

"Drizella! Anastasia!" the Stepmother shouted the next morning. "The Grand Duke is coming. He's searching for the girl who lost her slipper at the ball. The Prince wants to marry her."

Cinderella couldn't wait to try on the shoe. She went upstairs to get ready for the Grand Duke.

Suddenly, the Stepmother knew who the mysterious woman was at the ball. It was Cinderella! She laughed at the thought of Cinderella marrying a prince. Just as the Grand Duke arrived, the Stepmother locked Cinderella in her room and tucked the key safely in her pocket.

Jaq and Gus knew they had to help Cinderella.

As Drizella and Anastasia were trying on the shoe, Jaq and Gus crept down the stairs. They quietly slipped into the Stepmother's pocket and pulled out the key. Then they unlocked Cinderella's door.

Just as the Grand Duke was leaving, Cinderella raced down the steps.

"The girl is only a servant," the Stepmother said. "The shoe will not fit her."

"My orders are to try it on every maiden," the Grand Duke said. But just as he was handing the glass slipper to Cinderella, the Stepmother tripped him.

Crash! The tiny shoe shattered into little pieces.

The Grand Duke thought he'd never
find the right girl. But Cinderella smiled
sweetly. "I have the other slipper," she said, pulling it
out of her apron. Her stepmother gasped!

The Prince was delighted when he heard the news. He
and Cinderella were so in love they were married that very
day. As joyous wedding bells rang throughout the entire
kingdom, everyone celebrated the happy couple's true love.
Cinderella's dream had finally come true.